A Spell of

Kate Saunders worked as an actress until she was twenty-five and then became a writer. She has written five novels and edited a collection of short stories. As a journalist she has worked for the *Sunday Times*, the *Daily Telegraph*, the *Independent* and the *Sunday Express*, and is currently writing a weekly column in the *Express*. She can be heard regularly on BBC Radio 4, presenting *Kaleidoscope* and *Woman's Hour* and appearing on *Start the Week* and *Front Row*. She lives in London and has a six-year-old son.

The *Belfry Witches* titles are Kate's first books for children. A major BBC TV series is based on them.

Titles in The Belfry Witches series

All Belfry Witches titles can be ordered at
your local bookshop or are available by post
from Book Service by Post (tel: 01624 675137).

The Belfry Witches

A Spell of Witches

Kate Saunders
Illustrated by Tony Ross

MACMILLAN
CHILDREN'S BOOKS

For my son, Felix

First published 1999 by Macmillan Children's Books
a division of Macmillan Publishers Limited
25 Eccleston Place, London SW1W 9NF
Basingstoke and Oxford
www.macmillan.co.uk

Associated companies throughout the world

ISBN 0 330 37282 3

1 3 5 7 9 8 6 4 2

A CIP catalogue record for this book is available from
the British Library.

Typeset by SX Composing DTP, Rayleigh, Essex
Printed and bound in Great Britain by Mackays of Chatham plc, Kent

Contents

1

Red Stockings

"It's not fair!" moaned Old Noshie. "It's the unfairest thing in the world!"

"How dare she say we can't go to the Hallowe'en Ball?" raged Skirty Marm.

It certainly did seem very hard. On Witch Island, the Hallowe'en Ball was the high spot of the whole year. There was to be drink, food, dancing, a bonfire and a real jazz band. But Old Noshie and Skirty Marm – along with all the other Red-Stocking witches – had been ordered to stay in their caves.

I should explain that on Witch Island, when a witch reaches the age of one hundred, she is given her red stockings and uses the Red-Stocking Spellbook. At the age of two hundred, the stockings become green and the spellbook is more advanced. Finally, at the age of three hundred, a witch becomes a Purple-Stocking and is allowed to cast the most powerful spells of all.

Just because Mrs Abercrombie, the Queen of all the Witches, had heard some Red-Stockings tittering behind her back, she had decided they were silly and cheeky and should be punished. Their Red-Stocking Spellbooks were taken away for a week and they were banned from the Hallowe'en Ball. All the Red-Stockings were furious.

"What a nerve," said Skirty Marm, "treating us like little Yellow-Stockings!"

The Yellow-Stockings were the baby witches, still at school. It was a terrible insult.

The fact was, the Red-Stockings were not very popular among the senior witches – especially Old Noshie and Skirty Marm, who were often rather saucy and disrespectful. These two had been best friends since Yellow-Stocking days. They were now one hundred and fifty years old, which is very young for a witch.

Skirty Marm was tall and skinny, with a wrinkled grey face, beady red eyes and a tangle of purple hair. Old Noshie was shorter and fatter. Her face was bright green and glowed in the dark. She was bald but wore a blue wig to keep her head warm. On Witch Island, no witch gets a cave of her own until she is a Purple-Stocking, but Old Noshie and Skirty Marm were happy to share and had already decided that they would always live together.

They had been looking forward to the Hallowe'en Ball for months.

"It makes my blood boil!" said Old Noshie. "Let's have a nice cup of warm mud to cheer ourselves up."

Skirty Marm, however, was far too cross to think of being cheered up. "I don't care what Mrs Abercrombie says," she declared. "I'm going to that ball – whether she likes it or not!"

"Don't be daft," Old Noshie said. "Think what she'd do to you if she ever found out."

All the witches of Witch Island lived in terror of Mrs Abercrombie. The Queen of the Witches was hugely fat and amazingly ugly – even by witch standards. She had pointed iron teeth, her chin was covered with grey hairs, and she had a dreadful temper.

But more than this, Mrs Abercrombie owned the Power Hat. The Power Hat was two metres tall and had a candle stuck in the point at the top. The flame of this candle never went out, and the Hat gave its owner great magic powers. Nobody dared to annoy the queen when the Power Hat was on her head.

"I don't care," said Skirty Marm. "We're going to that ball, and Mrs A. won't know a thing. Listen . . ."

Grinning wickedly, she whispered her brilliant plan into Old Noshie's green ear.

Old Noshie was doubtful at first, but she always went along with Skirty Marm in the end. In her Yellow-Stocking days, her school reports had said she was "easily led", and this was still true where Skirty Marm was concerned – Old Noshie thought her friend was the cleverest witch in the world.

Hallowe'en is the night when the witches of the island fly out among the humans. They upset television aerials, prod sleeping babies to make them cry, and generally do all kinds of bad things. It is the witches' favourite night of the year – but this time, it was quite spoiled for the Red-Stockings.

As they lined up to mount their broomsticks, they looked sadly at the football pitch, which was decorated with coloured lights and black balloons, all ready for the party. Old Noshie and Skirty Marm, however, were in high spirits. They kept pinching each other and bursting into giggles, and nobody knew why.

It was a splendid night. Noshie and Skirty flew to a big city and made all the lights on tall office blocks spell out rude words. They went to a dairy and turned all the milk bad. They went to a flower market and changed all the flowers into mouldy cabbages.

At one hour past midnight, they landed on the black beach of Witch Island. The Hallowe'en Ball was in full swing. The football pitch was a

whirling mass of pointed hats and green and purple stockings. A gigantic bonfire filled the sky with a red glow, and the jazz band were playing wildly.

The Red-Stocking witches slunk miserably home to bed, pretending they didn't care. But Old Noshie and Skirty Marm rushed back to their cave, laughing so much that they could hardly stand up.

"Everything ready, Nosh?" asked Skirty Marm jauntily.

Old Noshie whispered, "Are you sure it will work?"

"Stop moaning," said Skirty Marm, "or I'll biff you. If we don't hurry, all the food will be gone – those old Purple-Stockings are such greedy pigs."

From under a rock she took two pairs of green stockings, which they had spent the whole afternoon dyeing in spinach juice. When they had put these on and admired their reflections in a puddle, they painted their faces so they would not be recognized. This was particularly important for Old Noshie, whose green face shone like a traffic light.

The moment their disguises were complete,

they ran out to the football pitch and threw themselves into the party. By now, the other witches were so tipsy that they hardly noticed these two strange Green-Stockings. Old Noshie and Skirty Marm hopped and jumped around the bonfire until they were breathless. Then they went to the food table and stuffed themselves with barbecued bats, salted newts' skulls and spiders in batter.

If they had been careful, they might never have been discovered. But it was at this point that the witches did a very silly thing. They grabbed a full bottle of Nasty Medicine and drank the whole lot between them, in five minutes.

Now, every sensible human knows you must NEVER, EVER drink someone else's medicine, because it is EXTREMELY DANGEROUS. But Old Noshie and Skirty Marm were witches, and all it did was make them disgracefully tipsy.

They looked over at Mrs Abercrombie, who was finishing a crate of Nasty Medicine single-handed. She was telling jokes which were not at all funny, but the crowd of Purple-Stockings around her had to laugh – they knew what a terrible temper she would be in the next day.

"It's time she was taught a lesson!" declared

Old Noshie. "Come on – it's my turn to have an idea for a change. I'll show her she can't squash us Red-Stockings!"

A few minutes later, the jazz band stopped playing and the lead singer made an announcement. "We're taking a break now while two talented Green-Stockings entertain you with a song. Here are the Bubbling Cauldron Stompers, wishing you a happy Hallowe'en!"

The crowd of witches clapped and whistled as a bald-headed Green-Stocking stepped onto the stage.

"My friend and I," she shouted, "will now sing a little song called 'A Nasty Old Thing'. Thank you."

Another Green-Stocking pranced onto the stage – but this time there was no applause. She had stuffed her dress with pillows to make her look very fat. She wore a false grey beard. Worst of all, she had a candle stuck in her pointed hat. The witches looked round at the queen, but Mrs Abercrombie was busy opening another bottle and had not seen the shocking figure on the stage.

In ghastly silence, the two talented Green-Stockings began to sing.

"Once there was an old witch,
O, harken to my tale,
She truly was a bold witch
And fatter than a whale.

Her chin was grey and hairy,
She snored just like a zombie –
O! Certainly no fairy
Was Mrs Abercrombie!"

A gasp of horror rose from the crowd, but the two Green-Stockings only sang louder.

"Her knees they were so baggy,
And (let us not quibble)
Her stomach was all saggy,
Her mouth was full of dribble.

From ten miles you could not miss her,
She's like a wobbly jelly –
I would not like to kiss her,
She is so Fat and Smelly!"

"Stop!" screamed Mrs Abercrombie. Her hideous face was as purple as her stockings. "How dare you insult your Beloved Queen?"

"Pooh to you!" smirked the two daring Green-Stockings.

"You'll be sorry for this!" roared Mrs Abercrombie, shaking a hairy fist. "What are your names?"

"Not telling!" shouted the two witches.

Mrs Abercrombie surveyed the crowd with a look that made them all tremble. "I want their names!"

Suddenly, one of the Purple-Stockings in the jazz band leapt onto the stage and grabbed Old Noshie by the ear.

"Look! This is a disguise – she's painted!"

"That's no Green-Stocking!" yelled someone else. "That's Old Noshie – I'd know her anywhere! And the other one must be Skirty Marm!"

"Arrest them!" bawled Mrs Abercrombie. "Throw them into prison! I shall try them tomorrow, in a Grand Court of Witches!"

"Oh, no!" wailed Old Noshie. "What have we done?"

And that is how Old Noshie and Skirty Marm committed the most terrible crime in the history of Witch Island.

2

No Stockings

"Silence in court," ordered Mrs Abercrombie. "Bring in the prisoners."

The Meeting Cave was packed. Every witch on the island had come to see the trial, and there had been fierce fighting for the best seats. The Yellow-Stockings – even little witches of only seventy or eighty – had been given the day off school. The Red-Stockings secretly felt rather proud of the two criminals, but the Green- and Purple-Stockings were furious.

When Old Noshie and Skirty Marm were led into the dock, the Green- and Purple-Stockings began to spit and shout and boo, and were only stopped by Mrs Abercrombie repeating, "Silence in court!"

There was silence at once, for the Queen of the Witches had never looked so terrifying.

"My subjects, last night, at the Hallowe'en

11

Ball, a shocking crime was committed against my sacred person."

"Woe!" cried the Green- and Purple-Stockings, "Woe to the prisoners!"

Old Noshie and Skirty Marm had their hands tied behind their backs, and they looked very sulky. They did not, however, look sorry for their shocking crime.

"Old Noshie and Skirty Marm," Mrs Abercrombie said, "you are charged with being at the Hallowe'en Ball without an invitation. You are also charged with unlawfully impersonating Green-Stockings, insulting your Beloved Queen – namely, me – and with being drunk and disorderly. Have you anything to say, before I find you guilty and punish you?"

"You were more drunk and disorderly than us!" said Old Noshie. "You had to be carried home."

"You are also charged with contempt of court!" screamed Mrs Abercrombie.

"Pooh to you!" replied the prisoners, sticking out their furry tongues at their Beloved Queen.

Mrs Abercrombie looked as if she would explode with rage. "Did you, or did you not, sing a

highly offensive song called 'A Nasty Old Thing'?"

"Yes," said Skirty Marm. "I wrote all the words, except the bit about you being fat and smelly – that was Noshie. We thought it was really funny."

"Funny!" gasped Mrs Abercrombie. "To insult *me*!"

"*Once there was an old witch*," chanted Old Noshie and Skirty Marm, "*O, harken to my tale – she truly was a—*"

Two Purple-Stocking guards stopped up their mouths with rags. The Meeting Cave was in an uproar. Several witches fainted with horror, and a dozen Red-Stockings had to be arrested for laughing.

"My subjects!" cried Mrs Abercrombie. "Are these rascals guilty or not guilty?"

"GUILTY!" cried thousands of witches with one voice.

"Right," said Mrs Abercrombie, "I will now pass sentence. And I will have such revenge as this island has never seen."

The crowd broke into murmurs of excitement. What would the queen do? The worst punishment on Witch Island was to have your broom broken in public, but there had never been a crime like this. Old Noshie and Skirty Marm were beginning to wish they hadn't been so cocky. They had decided they didn't care if their brooms were broken – but Mrs Abercrombie was looking ominously pleased with herself.

"Old Noshie and Skirty Marm," said Mrs Abercrombie solemnly, "you are sloppy, cheeky and disrespectful to your elders. You think you're going to get away with nothing worse than broken brooms – well, you aren't."

"No!" shouted all the older witches gleefully. "Certainly not!"

"If," the queen went on, "I have got my

temper back in a hundred years – which is VERY UNLIKELY – I may consider your case again. Meanwhile, for the crime of pretending to be Green-Stockings, you will be stripped of your red stockings for ever."

This was terrible. Old Noshie and Skirty Marm squealed inside their gags.

"And for the far more serious crime of singing that disgusting song, you will be banished from this island for one hundred years."

Old Noshie and Skirty Marm turned ashy pale. Banished! What would become of them?

The witches cheered Mrs Abercrombie out of the Meeting Cave, then surged away to listen to the highlights of the trial on the radio.

The two disgraced witches were locked up in prison until the hour of their banishment.

"This is all your fault," said Old Noshie. "I never should have listened when you made me gatecrash the ball."

"*My* fault?" shouted Skirty Marm. "We'd have been fine if you hadn't made me dress up as the queen!"

"We shouldn't argue," Old Noshie said, her green lip suddenly quivering. "We haven't got anything but each other now. Oh, Skirt, what's going to happen to us? Where will we go? Will we die?"

"I'm not going to die," growled Skirty Marm, trying to sound brave. "I wouldn't give Mrs A. the satisfaction. She'll be sorry for this one day, you mark my words."

When the night was at its blackest, Old Noshie and Skirty Marm were taken to the top of a high cliff and stripped of their red stockings.

"That'll teach you!" sneered the Purple-Stocking guard, waving the confiscated stockings in their faces. "You won't be so swaggering and cheeky now!"

Old Noshie and Skirty Marm had lost all their swagger and cheek. Now they were only cold and hungry, and very frightened. Struggling against the freezing wind, they mounted their broomsticks and flew out into the darkness.

Only a few hours before, they had ridden out for their Hallowe'en revels and thought it great fun. Now, they were leaving the only home they had ever known. It would be a hundred long years before they saw Witch Island again. Both of them sniffed, when they saw the sooty, rocky, ugly island falling away behind them.

Riding a broomstick is cold and uncomfortable at the best of times. Tonight, the wind howled around them, whipping their black rags and whistling through the holes in their pointed hats. They did not even have their red stockings to keep them warm.

Skirty Marm pressed the small radio button on her broom, which meant she could talk to Old Noshie over the roar of the wind.

"Cheer up, Nosh!"

Old Noshie pushed her radio button and said gloomily, "We'll have to live with the humans now. We'll probably get burnt."

"They haven't burned witches for hundreds of years," Skirty Marm said. "Most of them don't believe in us any more. And we've still got our magic powers."

"Yes," said Old Noshie, "but we haven't got our spellbooks."

"Oh, stop whining," Skirty Marm said crossly. "We can remember a few simple spells!"

"*You* can," sniffed Old Noshie. "You know I always have to look things up because I'm not as clever as you. I worked hard for those red stockings."

"Stop thinking about your stockings," said

Skirty Marm crossly. "We've got to decide where we're going. What about that big city where we played our Hallowe'en tricks?"

"I can't go that far," Old Noshie said in a wobbly voice. "I'm too hungry. I'd probably eat you on the way."

It took all their strength to fly now, for Mrs Abercrombie had summoned storm clouds to drive them far away from Witch Island. The bitter cold pinched their bones. Below them, they saw white-capped ocean waves, then cliffs, woods, fields and villages.

"You're good at geography," Old Noshie said. "Where are we?"

Skirty Marm frowned, trying to work it out without a map. "I think we're over a place called Hingland," she said. "They do morris dances and eat cake and drink lots of tea. Bit of a silly place by the sound of it."

"Look!" cried Old Noshie suddenly. "Over there – bats! Really juicy ones!"

The very word made their mouths water. Old Noshie was pointing to a tall stone tower with windows all round the top, and a pointed roof like a witch's hat. In the moonlight, bats swooped and fluttered around it.

Following the delicious bat smell, the two banished witches flew to the tower. They cheered up as soon as they landed in the gutter. Old Noshie put their brooms through one of the open stone windows for safe-keeping, and they settled down for a feast. They had not had a bite to eat since the ball and found the fat little bats very nourishing. When they were full, however, they realized how tired they were.

"I can't go any further," said Skirty Marm. "Let's have a sleep inside this tower."

"Right-ho," said Old Noshie.

They climbed inside and lay down on a dusty wooden floor. Skirty Marm used her hat as a pillow, and Old Noshie wrapped herself cosily in cobwebs.

"You know, Skirt," she yawned, "this isn't such a bad house. It reminds me rather of our cave." At the thought of their home (Cave 18, Stinker Street, Witch Island) she sighed. "What are we going to do for the next hundred years?"

"Well, there's one comfort about being banished," Skirty Marm said bravely. "We won't ever have to meet anyone as disgusting as Mrs Abercrombie again."

Exhausted by their horrible day, the witches fell asleep.

Little did they know that the storm clouds had blown them to someone every bit as disgusting as the queen – if not slightly worse.

3

A Bad Beginning

It was a fine, clear autumn Sunday in the little village of Tranters End. Mr Harold Snelling, the vicar of St Tranter's Church, and his poor curate, Mr Cuthbert Babbercorn, were sitting in the vestry before the service.

Mr Babbercorn was just taking a spoonful of Nasty Medicine, for his cough, when he heard a strange noise. It was a long, cackling, wicked laugh, somewhere above his head – and it gave him such a turn that he nearly dropped the medicine spoon.

"Did you hear that?" he gasped.

"Hear what?" Mr Snelling was busy eating a pork pie.

"I think," said Mr Babbercorn, "there's something cackling up in the belfry."

"Poor Cuthbert," said Mr Snelling kindly, "there's nothing up in that bell tower except a few bats. You're imagining things. I expect it's because Cousin Violet threw you downstairs again this morning."

Both men sighed deeply.

The vicar's Cousin Violet was known to everyone else as Mrs Bagg-Meanly. She kept house at the vicarage, and every soul in Tranters End was terrified of her. They quite understood why Mr Snelling hadn't dared to tell his distant cousin that he did not want a housekeeper. She had simply moved in, taking the best bedroom. She spent all Mr Snelling's money on herself and gave him such nasty food that the poor man was driven to keeping a secret supply – which she nearly always found. Only that morning she had discovered a couple of cheeses wrapped in his pyjamas and had locked them away in an iron safe in her bedroom, to eat herself.

The people of Tranters End felt very sorry for the vicar, but they were even sorrier for his young curate. If Mrs Bagg-Meanly underfed the vicar, she very nearly starved Mr Babbercorn. Though he was a good young man, she hated him and was full of plans to get rid of him. He was as thin as a stick and as pale as his own white collar, and his clothes were full of patches and darns. What little money he had of his own went on Nasty Medicine, for his cough. The village people would have loved to help him, but since Mrs Bagg-Meanly knew everything that went on, nobody dared.

"I often wonder," said Mr Snelling, "about what happened to her husband. If he ever existed."

"Perhaps she ate him," suggested Mr Babbercorn.

"If only something would happen to make her go away!" Mr Snelling sighed. "Then we'd all be free, and I could eat a decent meal at my own dining room table again. Yes, Mr Noggs?"

Mr Noggs, who was the churchwarden, had put his head round the vestry door.

"Excuse me, Vicar, Mrs Bagg-Meanly says it's time to start."

Mr Snelling and Mr Babbercorn jumped to it at once – they did not need to be told twice, with Mrs Bagg-Meanly glowering in the front pew. She was so fat, her corsets had be made specially, at a lorry factory. Her thin grey hair was squeezed into a mean, tight little bun. Her red face reminded people of a warty, bad-tempered toad.

Mr Babbercorn tried to keep very quiet and still during the service. Mrs Bagg-Meanly fined them for making illegal noises in church. He owed her a small fortune for coughing, and Mr Snelling was still paying off a fart by instalments.

Halfway through the service, Mr Babbercorn heard the cackling again. Stranger still, he began to hear a tune and words – something about an old witch who was fatter than a whale. He was sure he was not imagining things.

"I won't say a word to Mrs Bagg-Meanly," he said to himself. "I'll investigate this on my own."

25

As soon as the service was over, while Mr Snelling was busy asking people what they were having for lunch and Mrs Bagg-Meanly was putting the collection in her handbag, Mr Babbercorn took the key to the belfry from its rusty nail and crept round to the door.

There were one hundred and eighty-six steps up to the top of the tower, and by the time he reached the top he was breathless and dizzy. His heart was thumping as he opened the door into the bell loft. What would he find?

The belfry was empty. There were the four great windows with their giddy views across the countryside. There were the two great church bells. Nothing else – unless you counted dust and cobwebs.

"And yet," murmured Mr Babbercorn, "I could have sworn—"

"BOO!" screamed a voice behind him.

The curate spun round and saw . . .

"Witches!" He fell over, in a dead faint.

When Mr Babbercorn came to, he saw two faces peering down at him curiously. One was bright green, with a luminous glow. The other was framed with a tangle of purple hair. Both looked quite friendly, but unmistakably witchy.

"Are you a policeman?" asked the one with the green face.

"No, silly," said the other. "He's a dog. Look at his collar."

Mr Babbercorn sat up. "I'm not a dog," he said. "I'm a person. But what are you? I mean, are you – can you possibly be – genuine witches?"

"Course we are," Old Noshie said scornfully. "I'm Old Noshie and this is my pal, Skirty Marm. Who are you?"

"My name is Cuthbert Babbercorn," said Mr Babbercorn.

"Ha ha ha!" shrieked the two witches. "How silly!"

Privately, Mr Babbercorn thought this was rich, coming from creatures named Old Noshie and Skirty Marm. But he was too polite to say so. "I am the curate here," he explained. "That means a sort of assistant vicar."

"Of course!" yelled Skirty Marm. "We've landed in a church! We wondered why everyone was singing."

"We had a lovely time joining in," said Old Noshie.

"I know," Mr Babbercorn said. "I heard." How on earth was he to tell the vicar about this? Or Mrs Bagg-Meanly?

The witches were fascinated. They had heard about churches at Human Life classes when they were Yellow-Stockings. They bombarded Mr Babbercorn with questions, but he had plenty of his own.

"What are you two doing here? Don't you have a home?"

"No," Old Noshie said sadly. "We've been banished. We sang a rude song about our stinky old queen and we went to the ball when we hadn't been invited and we had our red stockings taken away and we won't be Green-Stockings for ages."

"And we're not sorry!" shouted Skirty Marm, shaking her fist.

Since Mr Babbercorn had not understood a word of this, the witches told him the whole story. They even sang him the song about Mrs Abercrombie, though they could hardly get the words out for laughing.

"I see," Mr Babbercorn said, amazed by this strange tale. "But you still haven't said how you got all the way up to the top of a locked tower."

"On our broomsticks, of course," said Skirty Marm.

"What broomsticks?" asked Mr Babbercorn.

"Why, over there—" began Old Noshie.

But there were no brooms to be seen.

"Aaargh!" bellowed Skirty Marm. "You've lost our brooms, you old fool! I'll squash your nose for this!"

"I put 'em through that window," protested Old Noshie. "I know I did."

They both went quiet as they thought about it.

"I know what it is," Skirty Marm said bitterly. "It's Mrs Abercrombie. She's used the Power Hat to call back our brooms."

"No brooms!" wailed Old Noshie. "Whatever shall we do? We were going to fly off to find a new home!"

"It looks as if you'll have to stay here," said Mr Babbercorn, trying not to sound as dismayed as he felt.

"We could train up some new brooms," said Skirty Marm, "if you show us the shop that sells Witches' Requisites."

"Gosh," said Mr Babbercorn, "I don't think we have a shop like that here."

"This is a nice place," Old Noshie announced. She took Mr Babbercorn's hand. "Will you be our friend?"

"With pleasure," said Mr Babbercorn. He was a kind-hearted man and he felt sorry for these two homeless witches. "But nobody must know you are here, and you must promise to behave. No turning people into frogs, for instance."

"Frogs?" Old Noshie said scornfully. "We haven't done that since we were Yellow-Stockings. It's baby stuff."

"Well, all right," said Mr Babbercorn. "If you are going to stay, I must warn you about the Curse of Tranters End."

With a deep sigh, he told the witches about Mrs Bagg-Meanly.

"Beware of her," he said. "She is wicked and mean and she will hate any friend of mine."

"We'll try very hard to be good," promised Skirty Marm. "It might be difficult at first, because we've never done it before. But we'll soon get the hang of it."

Mr Babbercorn got up from the floor and dusted himself down. "I must go," he said, glancing at his watch. "If I'm one second late for lunch, Mrs Bagg-Meanly puts it on the compost heap. I say – what will you two do about food?"

"We eat the bats," said Old Noshie. She plucked one out of her sleeve and ate it in a single gulp.

Mr Babbercorn wished he could fancy a bat. He was sure it would be more nourishing than Mrs Bagg-Meanly's cabbage pie.

"Goodbye, then," he said. "I'll come and see you tomorrow."

"What a nice human," said Old Noshie when he had gone. "And I'm looking forward to fixing up our new home."

"A few more cobwebs, a couple more mouldy patches, a touch of dry rot," said Skirty Marm happily, "and it could really look quite tasteful."

Old Noshie took a slurp of rainwater out of the gutter. "If only we had our spellbooks," she said.

"Pooh," Skirty Marm said, "stop going on about those."

"But, Skirt, how can we train up new broomsticks without them? I don't fancy being stuck here without a broom."

"I know the training spell by heart," said Skirty Marm. "I won a medal for broom-training at school, don't forget. We'll show Mrs A. she can't beat us!"

Remembering that their new friend had asked them to stay out of sight, the witches waited until the moon rose and the village was cloaked in darkness. Then they trotted down the one hundred and eighty-six belfry steps and into the high street. It was cold and drizzly and – luckily for the witches – not another soul was awake. At first, they walked about on tiptoe and were very, very good, for they had always wanted to get a close look at the way humans lived.

"What funny little birds," remarked Skirty Marm, looking at the ducks on the pond. "I wonder if they're nice to eat? We might get tired of bats."

Old Noshie was admiring a cluster of thatched cottages. "Why have those houses got hair?"

"Silly, that's not hair," said Skirty Marm. "That's their little hats, to keep off the rain."

They both sniggered, thinking the humans were very silly for not liking a drop of rain.

"Wow!" Skirty Marm said suddenly. "Look at this!"

She dragged her friend over to the window of

the Post Office and General Shop, and the two witches were so thrilled with what they saw there that they were quiet for nearly five minutes.

Crammed into the window were garden rakes, jars of sweets, aprons, babies' dresses, wellington boots, knitting wool, flower seeds and coloured postcards. Most interestingly of all, right at the back were two long BROOMS.

"Just what we need," whispered Skirty Marm. "We must take them at once and start work."

"Shouldn't we ask our new friend first?" Old

Noshie remembered Mr Babbercorn. "He said we had to behave."

"We'll ask him after we've nicked them," said Skirty Marm firmly.

She mumbled a spell and the post office window melted into mist. The two witches simply walked in, helped themselves to the brooms and hurried back to their belfry.

"Beautiful," said Skirty Marm when they were safely back in their new home. "Look at the workmanship. You don't get brooms like this on Witch Island."

"I nicked something else, too," Old Noshie said proudly. From under her rags, she pulled out a picture-postcard of the church. "Let's send it to Mrs A.!"

"Heeheehee!" cackled Skirty Marm. "I'd like to see her face when she gets it, the mean old slug!"

They wrote on the back of the card in Old Noshie's blood, which was dark green.

To old roten egg sumtimes known as Mrs Abercrombie Cave 1 Witch Island. Dere roten egg we R having a luvly time this is a piktur of our howse the wether is grate so POOH to you luv Old Noshie and Skirty Marm.

When they had stopped laughing, they sent this elegant message off to Witch Island, using a basic posting spell. Then it was time to tackle the far harder task of training their new broomsticks. Breaking in a broom is never easy. The witches did not have their spellbooks, and Skirty Marm's memory was not as good as she liked to pretend.

At first, they made all kinds of mistakes. Old Noshie changed the brooms into bicycles, which took ages to put right. Skirty Marm accidentally summoned a genie, who was very cross about being disturbed for nothing. Finally, after hours of wailing, quarrelling and biffing each other's noses, they managed to get the brooms to obey a few simple commands.

"Come on, let's go and find somewhere to practise," said Skirty Marm.

The two witches ran down the one hundred and eighty-six steps just as the sun was rising. In their excitement they had forgotten their promise to Mr Babbercorn, to stay out of sight.

4
Worse

In the high street, the sun had risen on a scene of panic. A crowd of people, all very excited, had gathered round the post office. Mrs Tucker, the postmistress, was sipping tea and telling her story to Constable Bloater, the local policeman.

". . . I came downstairs and there was my window. Or rather, there it wasn't . . ."

"Must've been a whole gang of them," said PC Bloater. "But what did they do with the broken glass? A whole window can't have vanished into thin air!"

Mr Snelling and Mr Babbercorn, who had heard the commotion, came running over from the vicarage.

"What's going on?" panted the vicar.

"There's been a robbery, that's what," said Mrs Tucker crossly.

"Dear, dear," said Mr Snelling, "what did they take?"

"That's the funny thing," said PC Bloater. "If you don't count the window, nothing but a postcard and two garden brooms."

"The old-fashioned sort," said Mrs Tucker, "like witches have in stories—"

"Oh, no!" squeaked Mr Babbercorn. At once, he guessed who was responsible.

Everyone turned to stare at him. Fortunately for the witches, however, they were distracted by the sound of a door slamming at the vicarage. The ground began to shake. A mighty voice boomed, "And *what*, may I ask, is the meaning of *this*?"

At once, everyone – even the ducks in the pond – fell silent. Up the street and through the little crowd stomped the enormous, terrible figure of Mrs Bagg-Meanly.

She wore a purple dressing gown, which exactly matched the colour of her toad-like face. Her thin, straggly hair was covered with a purple net. As it was early morning, she hadn't shaved and bristly grey hairs sprouted around her mouth.

"There . . . there's been a robbery, Cousin

Violet," faltered Mr Snelling.

"Who done it?" shouted Mrs Bagg-Meanly. "Nobody moves till I find out!"

"I'm taking care of things here," said PC Bloater weakly.

Mrs Bagg-Meanly's fist shot out. She knocked PC Bloater's helmet onto the ground. "Just because you wear a helmet, Bill Bloater, it don't make you Sherlock Holmes! I'll tell you what's going on. It's a plot, to upset my nerves. You'll all be sorry for this!"

Everyone trembled. They were sorry already.

It was at this moment that Mr Babbercorn happened to glance up at the church tower. What he saw made his heart sink. Two ragged black figures on broomsticks were whizzing round and round the steeple. In a moment, the whole village would know about the witches – and then what would happen to them?

Suddenly there was a resounding crash of breaking glass, as if a window had smashed in every single house in the village at the same time.

As they found out afterwards, this was exactly what had happened. Through each smashed window flew a stream of brooms, mops and brushes. The gaping villagers watched in stunned silence as their domestic implements glided gracefully down the high street.

PC Bloater was slightly grazed by his own lavatory brush, as it whistled past his ear. Eighteen mops got tangled in the telephone wires, which put the village telephones out of order for a week.

Mrs Bagg-Meanly squeaked, "My best big scrubbing-brush!" and fainted on top of Mr Babbercorn.

The brushes, mops and brooms turned the corner in neat formation and shot off in the direction of the motorway. They were never seen again and nobody ever found out what became of them.

There was a long silence, then Mr Snelling cleared his throat and said, "Did you all see that too?"

Immediately, realizing they had not gone mad, everyone began talking at once. What on earth had made their brooms and brushes fly away? Was it something to do with the ozone layer? Was it because Tranters End had been built on a mammoth's burial ground? Was it awesome science or fearsome magic?

"It was magic!" quavered Mrs Bagg-Meanly.

"Terrible magic!" She looked – very unusually – frightened. "Don't let it come near me!"

Then a little colour crept into her pale face. In her usual voice, she shouted, "I'm lying on something bony! Take it away!" From underneath her, Mr Snelling and PC Bloater pulled out the squashed, gasping figure of Mr Babbercorn.

"I might have known it was you, you nasty young man," grumbled Mrs Bagg-Meanly. "Don't you ever get underneath me again. It was like lying on a toast rack."

"Sorry," croaked Mr Babbercorn feebly.

The horrible housekeeper lumbered to her size eleven feet.

"I'm going for a lie-down till lunch," she announced, "so this village had better be quiet! If I'm disturbed . . ."

She did not need to finish the sentence. Her face looked so menacing that a deathly silence fell instantly. You could almost hear the beetles rustling in the grass. The size eleven feet went stomp-stomp-stomp back to the vicarage.

Mr Babbercorn wondered why Mrs Bagg-Meanly had looked so frightened – he hadn't expected her to believe in magic. He was not in the mood to wonder for long, however – there were far more urgent things on his mind. He was very much afraid that Old Noshie and Skirty Marm had more tricks up their ragged sleeves.

Mr Babbercorn was right – his witch troubles had only just begun. A little while earlier, Old Noshie and Skirty Marm had started training their new brooms in earnest. The two witches had found a deserted field where they hoped they could soon begin proper flying. Skirty Marm had some difficulty remembering all the right commands for novice brooms. Waking up every broom, mop and brush in the village had been her fault. Both the witches howled and screamed with laughter when they saw the procession of cleaning things hurtling down the street.

"You old silly," sniggered Old Noshie. "They'll all have to buy new ones now."

"Pooh," said Skirty Marm proudly. "These humans do far too much cleaning anyway. And I've remembered the proper spell now. Don't interrupt."

She mumbled a few words, and both witches shrieked with delight. The two brooms twitched, rose gently into the air, flew once round the field, then returned to be mounted.

"Good as gold," said Old Noshie, giving her broom a pat.

"Very comfy," said Skirty Marm as she mounted. "Not even Purple-Stockings have brooms as smart as these!"

There was a lot of wobbling and falling off at first, but before long the new broomsticks were behaving beautifully. That was when Old Noshie and Skirty Marm went whizzing round the steeple – they had quite forgotten their promise to stay out of sight.

"Whee! Look at me!" shouted Skirty Marm. She did a loop-the-loop, and both witches cackled when her hat fell off into a tree.

Old Noshie invented a brilliant new game. She flew high into the air and dropped her bright blue wig, and the witches had to catch it before it hit the ground. It was great fun. They were both in high spirits, and Skirty Marm was feeling particularly cocky.

"Look down there," she said, pointing to the crowd around the post office. "It's our friend, Mr B.! Shall we wave?"

"Better not. We promised to stay out of sight," said Old Noshie, feeling very virtuous.

"Let's go and have a good snoop around his house instead."

"Good idea," said Skirty Marm, pointing her broom towards the vicarage roof.

The vicarage, home of Mr Snelling, Mr Babbercorn and Mrs Bagg-Meanly, was a large, red-brick house, next to the church. The two witches hovered round the windows on their broomsticks, peeping in at all the rooms and enjoying themselves very much.

The first room they looked into was Mrs Bagg-Meanly's bedroom. It had a soft pink carpet, two cosy armchairs and a big iron safe in one corner. There was also a treacle tart on the windowsill. The witches had never seen a treacle tart before. They ate it and decided it was delicious.

The next window belonged to Mr Snelling's bedroom. This was not nearly so comfortable, but Old Noshie and Skirty Marm found several very interesting things which I shall come to later.

Last of all, they flew up to the attics and found the miserable little garret where Mr Babbercorn slept. The windows were broken. The floor was bare and full of splinters. The bed looked as hard as cement. And on the table stood a large brown bottle of . . .

"Hooray! Nasty Medicine!" cried Skirty Marm, snatching it greedily.

"Give us a swig, you old meanie!" roared Old Noshie, nearly toppling off her broom.

"No, I've got a better idea," said Skirty Marm. "Let's take it back to our tower and have a party. We can celebrate finding our new brooms."

Off the witches went, at the very moment Mr Babbercorn was being dragged out from under Mrs Bagg-Meanly. Shaken by the experience and worried that it would bring on his cough, he hurried up to his bedroom to take some Nasty Medicine.

"It's a mercy Mrs Bagg-Meanly didn't see the witches," he said to himself.

He looked on the table for his bottle of Nasty Medicine.

"Gone!" he cried. "Who would be wicked enough to steal my Nasty Medicine? Don't they know how DANGEROUS and STUPID it is to drink someone else's Nasty Medicine?"

Meanwhile, in the belfry, Old Noshie and Skirty Marm had finished the bottle. As I have said before, it is extremely DANGEROUS for humans to touch someone else's medicine. The witches were not humans, however, and all it did was make them shockingly tipsy.

"Let's have some fun, Nosh!" said Skirty Marm.

"What shall we do?" asked Old Noshie.

As usual, Skirty Marm was full of ideas. "Let's have a game of Vests-in-the-Rain."

Vests-in-the-Rain was a disgusting game, very popular among the Red-Stockings on Witch Island. You had to fly your broomstick over a washing line and spit at the washing below. If you hit an item of underwear, you got ten points.

There was a lot of underwear hanging out in Tranters End on this brisk, breezy day. Skirty Marm scored two hundred and eighty points. Old Noshie, who was not such a good shot, scored one hundred and sixty.

"I'm running out of dribble," she said eventually. "What shall we do now?"

"Let's have a sit-down on the vicar's roof," said Skirty Marm, "and shout rude things."

"Brilliant!" cried Old Noshie.

They flew over to the vicarage and perched comfortably on the sloping roof with their feet in the gutter. They did not have long to wait for the fun to begin.

Below them, they heard the booming voice of Mrs Bagg-Meanly.

"Harold Snelling! Have you been snooping in my bedroom?"

"Me, Cousin Violet?" squeaked the Vicar. "Never!"

"Then where," said Mrs Bagg-Meanly, "is my treacle tart?"

"I don't know, Cousin Violet. Honestly."

Up on the roof, the witches burst into giggles.

"I've made up one of my songs," said Skirty Marm. At the top of her voice, she began to chant:

"He did not eat your treacle tart,
He did not eat your pie,
He does not need to steal your grub
And here's the reason why."

"Where's that voice coming from?" yelled Mrs Bagg-Meanly. "Who's singing? Stop it, this instant, or I'll call the police!"
But the rude voice on the roof went on:

"I had a look inside his room
And found it full of eats;
He has a row of hollow books,
And fills them up with sweets!"

"Oh, they're *hollow*, are they?" said Mrs Bagg-Meanly menacingly. "I might have guessed."
"Please, Cousin Violet," begged poor Mr Snelling, "it won't happen again!"
On went the voice:

"What a funny man he is,
To fill the sink with bread!
There's jam tarts in his pillowcase
And biscuits in his bed!"

"I'd better take a look!" trumpeted Mrs Bagg-Meanly. "Stand aside, Harold!"

On the roof, Old Noshie said, "My turn!" She shouted:

"Behind a picture of his aunt,
There is some marzipan;
I think you'd better punish him –
He's such a greedy man!"

"Punish him?" said Mrs Bagg-Meanly. "I certainly will!"

The witches heard several thumps and crashes and muffled cries of "Ow!"

How could they? thought Mr Babbercorn, who had of course been listening. "Poor Mr Snelling – he's been hoarding that secret food for weeks!" And he burst into a fit of coughing.

The last thing the witches heard, as they wobbled back to their belfry, was Mrs Bagg-Meanly shouting, "Don't you corf at me, young man! I will not have corfing!" Followed by more thumps and crashes.

The witches were not sorry for the trouble they had caused. They were feeling very tired now and all they wanted to do was sleep.

Three hours later, when Mr Babbercorn climbed the one hundred and eighty-six steps up to the belfry and opened the door, a very vulgar scene met his eyes.

Old Noshie and Skirty Marm lay snoring on the floor with their hats over their eyes. The two stolen brooms lay in one corner with the empty bottle of Nasty Medicine between them.

"Witches," said Mr Babbercorn sternly, "wake up at once!"

Old Noshie and Skirty Marm took their hats off their faces and groaned.

"I feel terrible!" wailed Skirty Marm. "I'll never touch another drop as long as I live!"

"Hello, Mr B.," said Old Noshie. "Have you come to cheer us up?"

"Certainly not!" said Mr Babbercorn. "I've been squashed flat, Mr Snelling has had his secret food taken away, the whole village is in an uproar – and it's all your fault!"

49

"Well, of all the cheek," Old Noshie said huffily. "What have *we* done?"

"You stole two brooms," Mr Babbercorn said. "You flew about on them in broad daylight. You broke windows all over Tranters End and made all the mops and brushes escape. You sang a dreadful song, which got the vicar into trouble with Mrs Bagg-Meanly. You zoomed about spitting on people's washing – oh, yes, you did. I saw you, and it's a miracle nobody else did. Worst of all, you stole my Nasty Medicine – even though drinking someone else's medicine is extremely WICKED and DANGEROUS. Oh, witches! How could you be so naughty?"

The witches hung their heads.

"I want to be your friend," said Mr Babbercorn, "but I don't see how I can be if you're going to behave like this."

"We didn't mean to be naughty," mumbled Skirty Marm. "We were only having a bit of fun."

"We got you into trouble when we promised to be good!" cried Old Noshie, bursting into tears. And they both began to wail and sob and howl until Mr Babbercorn was afraid someone would hear.

"Be quiet!" he hissed. "I'll forgive you, if you swear you'll give up your bad, witchy ways and try hard to be good."

"We will!" they cried. "We'll try ever so hard! Please don't stop being our friend!"

Mr Babbercorn took out his handkerchief and blew his nose. He was very touched by the witches' repentance. "We'll say no more about it then. We'll start all over again. Goodbye, witches." He hurried away down the one hundred and eighty-six steps.

Old Noshie and Skirty Marm were sadder and wiser witches now.

"Noshie," said Skirty Marm in a solemn voice, "from tomorrow we'll be so good our new friend will hardly recognize us."

5

Shrinking Violet

Next morning, the witches woke before dawn and remembered this was the first day of their new life of Virtue. They were rather depressed.

"Blimey," complained Skirty Marm, "how do you go about being good? Can you remember anything about being good in our spellbooks, Nosh?"

"Nope," said Old Noshie. "All they said was how to be bad. That was the whole point."

They thought very hard and decided to start by mixing Mr Babbercorn some new Nasty Medicine for his cough. This was tricky without their spellbooks, but Skirty Marm was sure she remembered the recipe. As the sun rose, they flew over the fields collecting herbs and berries. Then they boiled them up in rainwater – using Old Noshie's hat as a saucepan – and poured the mixture into Mr Babbercorn's medicine bottle.

"Skirt," said Old Noshie in a worried voice, "I don't remember it being pink . . . Are you sure you've got it right?"

Skirty Marm was not very sure, but said crossly, "Of course it's right, you old fool. Anyway, it's prettier than the old stuff. I bet he'll be pleased."

After checking there was nobody about, the two witches flew over to the vicarage and left the bottle on Mr Babbercorn's windowsill. They waited in a mulberry tree nearby for him to find it.

"I've thought of something else," said Old

Noshie. "Is a witch cough the same as a human cough?"

"All right, smelly!" shouted Skirty Marm. "Make it yourself if you're so clever!"

"Sorry," mumbled Old Noshie.

"Shhh!" whispered Skirty Marm. "Here he comes!"

But it was not Mr Babbercorn. Mrs Bagg-Meanly stomped into the curate's bedroom to polish the floor, hoping he would slip and break something. To the horror of the witches, she walked straight over to the bottle of Nasty Medicine. The autumn sun, suddenly bursting through the clouds, lit it up like a pink jewel.

"Hmmm," said Mrs Bagg-Meanly, "this isn't the stuff the little beast usually takes!" She took out the cork and sniffed it suspiciously. "Delicious! Far too good for the likes of him!"

And she swigged the whole lot, in one big gulp.

"Greedy pig!" wailed Skirty Marm, "Now we'll have to make some more!"

"Skirt!" gasped Old Noshie. "Look!"

A strange expression was creeping over Mrs Bagg-Meanly's face – as well it might, for something awful was happening to her.

"Help! Police!" she screamed. "I'm SHRINKING!"

And so she was. Her mighty voice was shrinking, too, until it was hardly more than a mouse's squeak.

"Told you it was the wrong potion," Old Noshie whispered. "What a good thing Mr B. didn't drink it."

Mrs Bagg-Meanly's little head vanished beneath the edge of the table, and the two witches laughed so hard they had to clutch their brooms to stop themselves falling out of the tree.

"Let's go and take a look at her," said Skirty Marm.

They squeezed themselves and their broomsticks through Mr Babbercorn's broken bedroom window. Mrs Bagg-Meanly was now about the size of a teacup. The witches laughed even harder and this made Mrs Bagg-Meanly very angry.

She shook her tiny fist at them. "If you two are responsible for this, you put me right at once!"

"Heeheehee!" tittered Skirty Marm. "Impossible!"

"We don't know how!" sniggered Old Noshie.

This was quite true. The antidote to the spell was in the Red-Stocking Spellbook – which, of course, they didn't have.

"You'll suffer for this. I have connections," raged Mrs Bagg-Meanly. "Nobody does magic on me and gets away with it!"

She bit Old Noshie's toe.

"Ow!" complained Old Noshie. "She's ever so vicious, Skirt. Put her in the medicine bottle and cork her up tight."

"Good idea," said Skirty Marm.

Mrs Bagg-Meanly kicked and screamed, but to no avail. She was rammed down the neck of the bottle and corked up in her glass prison.

"Skirt," Old Noshie said uneasily, "will Mr Babbercorn be pleased about this?"

"Deary me," said Skirty Marm, "he ought to be. But he's such a funny little thing – he might say we've been naughty."

"And I've thought of something else." Old Noshie sounded scared. "Suppose the spell wears off? Think what she'll do to him when she grows again!"

They stared at each other, dismayed. What had they done? And at that very moment, they heard Mr Babbercorn coming up the stairs. The cowardly witches did not dare to face him. They jumped on their brooms and fled back to the belfry.

When Mr Babbercorn entered his bedroom, the fateful bottle was the first thing he saw.

"I do believe those witches have mixed me some new medicine!" he said. "How kind!"

But when he picked up the bottle, he got one of the worst shocks of his life.

"It can't be!" he gasped. "I must be seeing things!"

Inside the bottle, tiny Mrs Bagg-Meanly was stamping her little feet. Mr Babbercorn looked out of the window – just in time to glimpse a guilty green face in the belfry.

Very carefully, he took out the cork.

"Wait till I grow again!" shrilled the little voice. "You'll be sorry you was ever born!"

"I'm afraid there's nothing I can do," Mr Babbercorn said, quite kindly. "There's been a dreadful mistake."

He popped the cork back, wondering what to do.

"I'll tell the vicar," he decided. "He's such a sensible man."

Holding the bottle very carefully, he went

down to Mr Snelling's study.

"Excuse me, Vicar," he said. "I have to speak to you urgently. It's about Mrs Bagg-Meanly."

"Keep your voice down!" hissed Mr Snelling. "She'll hear you!"

"She won't," said Mr Babbercorn. "Something has happened to her. Something terrible."

Mr Snelling's face became bright with hope. "Has she gone to live with her sister?"

Mr Babbercorn said, "I'm holding her in my hand."

Amazed, Mr Snelling stared into the bottle and saw Mrs Bagg-Meanly's toad-like mouth opening and shutting.

"Good gracious," he said, "it's Cousin Violet!"

"I can't quite explain how," said Mr Babbercorn, "but a spell has been cast on her. I was hoping you'd know what to do."

"DO?" shouted the vicar. "Are you mad? She's shut in a bottle and she can't get out! Oh, joy! Oh, rapture!"

He did a little dance and kissed Mr Babbercorn on the nose.

"This is the happiest day of my life! Tell you what, Cuthbert, we'll have a feast of my secret food to celebrate. And Cousin Violet can watch us eat it!"

"But Vicar . . ." began Mr Babbercorn. "What if she grows back again?"

"Nonsense!" sang Mr Snelling. "Don't be such a wet blanket!"

He crouched down and stuck his tongue out at the bottle. Mrs Bagg-Meanly danced with fury, but there was nothing she could do.

"Cuthbert," Mr Snelling said briskly, "run round to Mrs Noggs and tell her we can't come to the jumble sale meeting. I'll get the lunch."

Mr Babbercorn ran out at once. He did not, however, go to Mrs Noggs. Up the one hundred and eighty-six steps to the belfry he pelted, and found Old Noshie and Skirty Marm hiding their guilty faces in their hats.

"I want an explanation!" he said sternly.

"Don't be cross," moaned Old Noshie. "It was a mistake!"

"I'm sure you meant well," said Mr Babbercorn, "and I'll admit I am tempted to leave her in the bottle. But you can't go round casting spells on people. You must put it right at once."

"We can't remember how," Skirty Marm said

forlornly. "But we have remembered something." She did not dare to look Mr Babbercorn in the eye. "The . . . the spell wears off at sunset."

"No!" groaned Mr Babbercorn. "Oh, witches, witches, what shall I do? No, don't start crying! You've got to think of a way to put this ghastly mess right."

"Forgive us!" begged the weeping witches.

"Yes, yes – just do what you can." And Mr Babbercorn rushed back to the vicarage.

He found Mr Snelling spreading his secret food across the dining room table. The vicar was in a festive mood – he was singing, and he had tied one of Mrs Bagg-Meanly's elastic stockings in a bow round his bald head.

"Vicar," began Mr Babbercorn, "I'm afraid I've got some rather worrying—"

"Honestly, Cuthbert," said Mr Snelling, "what an old fusspot you are! Sit down and eat, before these lovely chips go cold."

"But we can't—"

"Have a smartie." The vicar pushed his curate into a chair and made a hideous face at the bottle.

Inside it, the rage of the teeny Mrs Bagg-

Meanly was a terrible thing to behold.

Sunset! thought Mr Babbercorn. It's November and it'll be dark in no time! Suppose the witches can't do anything?

He looked at the delicious food on his plate. There were chips, beefburgers, pork pies, chocolate cakes and loads of sweets. Mr Babbercorn was very hungry and ate every crumb. But the feast was quite spoiled by the sight of the sun sinking slowly outside the dining-room window.

Mr Snelling ate and ate, until the red sun was just on the point of dipping into the horizon.

"Lovely," he declared, wiping chocolate off his mouth. "Best meal I ever had."

Mr Babbercorn cleared up the crumbs and took the dirty plates to the kitchen. Where, oh where were Old Noshie and Skirty Marm when he needed them? He washed the dishes quickly and hurried back to the dining room.

The vicar had let Mrs Bagg-Meanly out of the bottle and was making her jump over his finger while she scampered furiously across the table.

"You'll be sorry for this, Harold Snelling!" she squeaked in her tiny voice.

"Silly old Cousin Violet!" giggled Mr Snelling. "What can you do to me?"

"I'll tread on your glasses . . . I'll burst your hot-water bottle . . . I'll bite your ears until you beg for mercy—"

"Back in your bottle, Cousin Violet, dear!" sang Mr Snelling.

But at that moment, the sun sank below the horizon. Mr Babbercorn's spirits sank with it. Too late!

"Aaarrgh!" screamed the vicar.

Mrs Bagg-Meanly was grinning now, for she was growing larger every second. First, she was the size of the medicine bottle, then she was the size of a chair, and in no time she was her old self again – standing on the table with her arms folded.

"Well, well, well," she said, "what a LOVELY day you've had, Harold."

"Cousin Violet . . ." It was the vicar's turn to squeak now. "I can explain—"

"And YOU!" she roared at Mr Babbercorn. "You little squirt! You horrible, sneaking little runt! When I've finished with you, you won't have a whole bone left! I'll send you back to the bishop in an envelope!"

Mr Babbercorn trembled, but suddenly saw two witchy faces peeping over the windowsill. He heard two voices muttering a spell. He held his breath.

A look of bewilderment dawned on Mrs Bagg-Meanly's face. "Where am I?" she croaked. "What am I doing standing on the table? Help me down . . . I've come over all queer . . . I don't remember a thing . . ."

She was pale green and shaking. The vicar and Mr Babbercorn helped her down from the table, and she did not even try to hit them. Groaning softly, she tottered away to her bedroom.

For several minutes, Mr Snelling and Mr Babbercorn stood in dazed silence.

"She's . . . she's lost her memory," Mr Babbercorn said. "We're safe."

He made a pot of tea with two teabags left over from the feast, and they sat down to recover from their fright.

"It was a lovely day," sighed Mr Snelling presently. "And what a lucky escape we had – I was just about to mix a trifle in her best hat!"

Very quietly, they laughed.

The only reminder of that strange afternoon was a row of tiny footprints in the butter.

6

Mr Babbercorn's Birthday

After the shrinking incident, the rest of November passed peacefully in Tranters End. Old Noshie and Skirty Marm worked hard at being good – even when Mr Babbercorn insisted that being good meant no more magic.

"But some of our spells are very kind!" argued Skirty Marm.

"If you want to live in this village," Mr Babbercorn said firmly, "you have to behave like humans. And that means no spells at all. Even kind ones. No more swooping about on your brooms in broad daylight. And definitely no more games of Vests-in-the-Rain."

"Oh, well," said Old Noshie, "we'll do our best. We don't want to get banished again."

There was one bad incident when they turned the parrot on Mrs Tucker's best hat into a vulture. On the whole, however, the two witches were doing well. They began to settle into a routine, staying in their belfry when it was light and only flying out on their brooms when darkness fell.

Skirty Marm sometimes moaned that being good was boring, but she wanted to stay in Tranters End. There were lots of things about the village that she liked very much – for instance, when the great church bells rang on Sunday mornings. Humans would have found the noise in the belfry unbearable, but the witches loved the din and had great fun riding on the bells as they rocked to and fro.

Best of all, they had a real friend. Mr Babbercorn climbed the one hundred and eighty-six steps nearly every day to drink warm rainwater with the witches and listen to their tales of Witch Island. He had grown very fond of Old Noshie and Skirty Marm and often thought how lonely he would feel without them.

One morning, in early December, when the woods and fields were white with the first snow, Old Noshie said to Skirty Marm, "Skirt, I wish we had some money. Today is Mr Babbercorn's birthday. Wouldn't it be nice to give him a present?"

"Oh yes, let's," said Skirty Marm. "Poor thing – he gets weedier every day. Even his delicious Nasty Medicine doesn't seem to do him any good. That stinky Mrs Bagg-Meanly is starving him, when he should be having a lovely tea party."

The curate had told them all about human birthdays, and they were very sorry they could not give him a cake with candles on – they thought this sounded wonderful. Birthdays were never noticed on Witch Island, unless a witch was moving into new stockings. Even then, nobody had much fun.

"Maybe we could nick something?" suggested Old Noshie.

Skirty Marm shook her head. "He'd only get cross, and we don't want that. But I've had a brilliant idea!"

While the witches were planning his birthday, Mr Babbercorn was chopping wood in the vicarage garden, blowing on his fingers to stop them turning blue with cold. He was quite alone. Mrs Bagg-Meanly had gone shopping for the day, and Mr Snelling had a jumble sale meeting.

Mrs Bagg-Meanly had been careful to lock up every crumb of food, and Mr Babbercorn had not had a bite to eat for two days. He was so hungry he had even tried eating a used teabag he had fished out of the dustbin.

"I don't think I've ever been so miserable," he said to himself. "Never mind, when I've finished here I'll go and call on the witches. They always cheer me up."

He raised the axe to make another chop, and gasped, "Ow!"

Something extremely peculiar was happening. The ground fell away under his feet, the axe dropped from his hand, and he found himself floating high in the air with his chin resting on the Vicar's bedroom windowsill.

"Goodness," he exclaimed, "I appear to be – flying!"

A gust of wind blew him over the chimney in a perfect somersault. He flew out over the high street like a kite.

Below him, Mrs Tucker and Mrs Noggs were sweeping their garden paths.

"Well I never," remarked Mrs Tucker, "there goes Mr Babbercorn!"

"Poor young dear," said Mrs Noggs from the other side of the fence. "I always said he was an angel."

"What shall I do?" wondered Mr Babbercorn. "Perhaps I should ask Mrs Noggs to call the fire brigade. How long will I be stuck up here?"

His question was answered by another gust of wind. A moment later, he was sitting on the floor of the belfry with his glasses hanging off one ear.

"Hahahaha!" shrieked Old Noshie and Skirty Marm.

"I might have known you two would be at the bottom of this," said Mr Babbercorn, trying to look strict. "What are you up to?"

"Happy birthday to you!" bawled the witches. "Happy birthday to you, happy birthday DEAR CUTHBERT, happy birthday to you!"

"It's my birthday!" cried Mr Babbercorn. "I quite forgot!"

"And we've got a present for you," said Skirty Marm. "You're going to have a holiday."

"Now that you can fly," Old Noshie said, "we're going to take you somewhere lovely – only you mustn't ask where because it's a surprise."

"I don't suppose it would matter," Mr Babbercorn said thoughtfully, "just for one day.

Why not? I haven't had a holiday for years. I'm sure it would do me good."

"Hurrah, that's settled then!" crowed Skirty Marm. "Follow us!"

She grabbed Mr Babbercorn's hand, and he was slightly alarmed to find himself being pulled out of the window. They came out above thick clouds, soaking wet and very cold. Clutching the back of Old Noshie's broomstick, the curate flew higher and higher, faster and faster.

After a while, he noticed he was getting warmer. At first, he thought this must be because of the effort of holding onto the broom, but presently he became so hot that he took off his jacket, then his scarf, then his pullover. Though he had no clue where he was, he realized how fast they were going when they overtook an aeroplane. He just had time to glimpse the astonished face of the pilot, before they left it far behind.

Suddenly the clouds melted away and he was gazing down at a deep blue sea, winking like a sheet of sapphire in the blazing sun.

"We're here!" cried Old Noshie.

The warm air rushed around him, and Mr Babbercorn landed on something beautifully

soft. He opened his eyes and was speechless with delight. They were on a long, white beach with waves lapping gently at the sand, tall palm trees and scented groves of fruit.

While he gazed around, the witches watched him anxiously.

"Well?" asked Skirty Marm. "Do you ... do you like it?"

"Oh, witches, it's perfect!" said Mr Babbercorn. "It's the best birthday present I ever had!"

Old Noshie blushed dark green with pleasure, and Skirty Marm's purple hair crackled with pride. They had never given anyone a present before (there was no such thing on Witch Island) and they liked the feeling extremely.

"Let's have lunch," said Old Noshie.

Flying from tree to tree on their broomsticks, the two witches gathered piles of coconuts, pineapples, oranges, dates and bananas. They all ate until they were full and sticky with juices.

Mr Babbercorn could hardly believe his luck. Only that morning he had been slaving in the vicarage garden. Now here he was, sunbathing on a desert island.

Bless these witches, he thought. How glad I am that they came to Tranters End.

All that long afternoon they played games in the sand, paddled in the sea, or simply lay basking in the shimmering heat. They made a sandcastle using the witches' hats as buckets. Noshie and Skirty taught Mr Babbercorn to play Witch Football, with an invisible ball, and magicked up a rather mouldy-tasting birthday cake.

At last, when the tropical sun was turning red, Mr Babbercorn sighed and said, "I'm afraid it's time we were getting back." He could not help looking sad as he fastened on his curate's collar.

They all sat quietly, thinking of the wintry village, the icy vicarage and wicked Mrs Bagg-Meanly.

"We won't let you go back!" blurted Skirty Marm. "We'll stay here for ever!"

"We can build a nice little house in a tree," Old Noshie said comfortably. "Won't that be fun?"

Mr Babbercorn shook his head. "I'm sorry, witches. You may stay here, but I must go home."

"Why?" asked Skirty Marm. "You don't like it."

"Humans have to do lots of things they don't

like," Mr Babbercorn explained. "I am the curate at Tranters End – which means the people need me, not to mention poor Mr Snelling. It would be awfully mean of me to leave him alone."

"Deary me," said Old Noshie in a disappointed voice, "how horrid it is, being good."

Skirty Marm had a worrying thought. "I say – you do want us to come back with you, don't you?"

Mr Babbercorn laughed. "Of course. You're my best friends."

The witches beamed, feeling very honoured.

"We'll come home then," she announced. "I would have missed our tower, anyway."

"Hmph," muttered Old Noshie crossly. She had been looking forward to setting up house in a tree.

"I'll tell you a human saying," said Mr Babbercorn. "It goes like this: *East, West, Home's Best.* Even when it's not perfect, or even very nice, it's still home."

Old Noshie brightened. She could never stay in a bad mood for long. "It won't be so bad, if we take some fruit back with us."

The two witches filled their hats with fruit, and Mr Babbercorn tucked the biggest pineapple he could find inside his jacket as a present for the vicar. When darkness began to fall across that lovely island, they all flew home.

More snow had fallen during the afternoon, and the air was crisp with frost. By the light of the moon, holly berries glowed scarlet among their spiked green leaves.

Mr Babbercorn yawned when the three of them landed in the belfry.

"I can't thank you enough for this gorgeous day," he said. "I feel ten years younger!"

"I wish we could do it every day," Old Noshie said sadly.

"Cheer up, Noshie!" said Mr Babbercorn. "Think what fun you'll have in all this snow. You've never seen proper, thick snow before. Tomorrow, I'll tell you how to make a toboggan."

Old Noshie and Skirty Marm thought a toboggan sounded brilliant, and when Mr Babbercorn went away down the one hundred and eighty-six steps he left two very contented witches behind him.

"Didn't he look happy, Skirt?" mused Old

Noshie as she mulled over the glories of the day. "Wasn't it great, to see him smile and play?"

"Tell you what, Nosh," said Skirty Marm, "I'm beginning to see the point of this being good lark. I think it has something to do with the lovely feeling you get when you make a nice person happy. If this is being good, I like it!"

The next morning, Mr Babbercorn and Mr Snelling sat at breakfast in the kitchen while Mrs Bagg-Meanly ate a private (and much bigger) breakfast in the dining room. Mr Snelling counted out the ten cornflakes they were each allowed and rustled his newspaper.

"Here's a funny story," he said. "Listen to this: 'I Saw Flying Parson Claims Airline Pilot.' What next, eh?" He glanced up at Mr Babbercorn. "Goodness, Cuthbert, how well you look. If it wasn't December, I'd say you had a suntan!"

Mr Babbercorn whispered, "I've got a pineapple for you."

"A pineapple!" gasped Mr Snelling. "Where did you get a pineapple?"

"Ask no questions," said Mr Babbercorn with a meaningful wink, "and you'll be told no lies."

7

The Divine Floradora

Christmas was coming, and Old Noshie and Skirty Marm were intensely interested in all the preparations. They had never known such a thing on Witch Island where Christmas was a day like any other. The kindly curate found some mouldy old paper chains and gave them to the witches to decorate the belfry. They were already very busy, catching bats and mixing potions for their special Christmas lunch.

Every night Old Noshie and Skirty Marm flew round the sleeping village, admiring the tinsel in the shops and peeping at everyone's Christmas trees.

One night, they found a large notice on the door of the church hall.

"'Christmas Concert at Tranters End'," read Skirty Marm. "'Come One, Come All for an Evening of Village Talent. Performers Welcome'."

"A concert!" cried Old Noshie. "What a treat! I'd love to a see a concert!"

"I've got a better idea," said Skirty Marm, who always had a better idea. "We should be in it. We could sing 'A Nasty Old Thing'. Wouldn't they all roll about laughing? Let's ask Mr Babbercorn."

But Mr Babbercorn did not like the idea at all.

"Certainly not!" he snapped. Seeing they were disappointed, he said, more gently, "Think of the fuss there would be when people saw two witches."

Old Noshie and Skirty Marm scowled.

"Nobody needs to know we live here!" argued Skirty Marm. "You could just pretend we're witches from another village."

"Other villages don't *have* witches," said Mr Babbercorn. "It's out of the question."

"Meanie!" shouted Old Noshie. "You never want us to have any fun!"

"I'm sorry, Noshie," said Mr Babbercorn, "but you must promise me not to set foot inside the church hall during the concert."

Both witches set up a howl of protest at this so he added, "I might let you watch it through the skylight in the roof – but only if you promise to be good."

Sulkily, both witches promised.

"I do hope they behave," he said to himself when he left them. "It's been so peaceful lately."

He would not have been at all happy if he had heard the conversation in the belfry after he had gone.

"That smelly spoil-sport!" grumbled Old Noshie. "Now we won't have our treat."

But Skirty Marm – that witch of great ideas – was busy thinking. Presently, she said, "There is a way we could do something at the concert."

"No, there isn't," Old Noshie said with a

sniff. "Not now we've promised to stay out of the hall."

"We don't have to go into the hall!" cackled Skirty Marm. "Listen . . . "

And she whispered her plan into Old Noshie's green ear.

Two days later, when Mr Snelling and Mr Babbercorn were sorting out the programme for the concert, Mr Snelling said, "Here's a funny thing, Cuthbert."

"What?" Mr Babbercorn was working at the typewriter.

"It's a letter from Ted Blenkinsop over at Blodge Farm." The vicar put on his glasses, to read it. "'Dere Mr Sneling I want to be in the consert. Pleese put me in as the Divine Floradora. Luv Mr Blenkinsop.' Most odd, don't you think? And the spelling is dreadful."

Mr Babbercorn was too busy to pay much attention. "Ted Blenkinsop," he said as he typed out the programme, "as the Divine Floradora."

On the night of the concert, every soul in Tranters End was packed into the hall. They wouldn't have missed this social pinnacle for the world, even if Mrs Bagg-Meanly had not ordered them all to turn up. The evil housekeeper was checking their names on a list as they came in.

Old Noshie and Skirty Marm were at the back door of the church hall, dancing with excitement. Hidden in the bushes beside them was a large, black shape.

"Do you remember what to do?" whispered Skirty Marm. "When Mrs Tucker plays your music, you dance onto the stage—"

"Of course I remember," said the mysterious shape in the bushes. "Don't fluster me."

"Come on, Skirt," nagged Old Noshie. "Let's get up on the roof before it starts."

The two witches climbed up the drainpipe and peeped through the skylight in the church hall roof, pinching each other with wicked glee.

Mr Babbercorn was standing beside the door, ready to switch off the lights.

That's strange, he thought suddenly. There's Ted Blenkinsop in the front row! Surely he's meant to be performing?

A horrible thought came into his head. He glanced up at the skylight and, to his relief, saw Old Noshie's glowing green face. No, it couldn't be anything to do with the witches. All the same, it was peculiar. Ted Blenkinsop was a stout man with a red face and a bald head. It was difficult to imagine him as the Divine Floradora. Or, indeed, as the Divine anything.

But there was no time to solve the mystery. Mr Snelling was signalling from behind the curtain. Mr Babbercorn switched off the lights. The show was beginning.

Mr Snelling loved the concert. He started it, as he did every year, by singing 'When Father Papered the Parlour', with Mrs Tucker playing the piano. The audience clapped very loudly. They were fond of their vicar and this was the only way they dared to show it.

Next, Mrs Bagg-Meanly sang 'Sweet and Low', timing the applause afterwards with her watch.

"This is it! This is it!" hissed Old Noshie.

"Ladies and gentlemen," announced Mr Snelling, "please welcome the Divine Floradora!"

Mrs Tucker struck up the music. With a loud clatter, the Divine Floradora took the stage.

"Oh my goodness!" choked Mr Snelling. There were gasps and whispers all round the church hall.

The Divine Floradora wore a silk garter on one leg and a pink rose behind one ear. She also wore scarlet lipstick and false eyelashes. Old Noshie and Skirty Marm had to pinch each other black and blue to stop laughing out loud. The Divine Floradora was a LARGE BROWN COW.

There was an even greater sensation when she stopped dancing and began – in a deep contralto voice – to sing.

"Who dances like a fairy?
Floradora!
Who is beautiful, though hairy?
Floradora!
Who dresses up in silk
And gives champagne instead of milk?
I'm referring to the lovely
Floradora!

"Who mouldered in her field
(Floradora!)
Till she practically congealed?
Floradora!
Who escaped one day for good
And went off to Hollywood?
It could only be the gorgeous
Floradora!"

The church hall seethed with excitement. The people at the back stood on their chairs to get a better view. Mr Snelling's mouth gaped open in amazement. Even Mrs Bagg-Meanly was silent.

"What on earth shall I do?" wondered Mr Babbercorn, for of course he knew who was behind this outrage.

Mrs Tucker had stopped playing the piano, but the Divine Floradora, enjoying the attention, went on kicking her front legs and stamping her hoofs.

Mrs Bagg-Meanly had recovered. She stomped onto the stage.

"Right," she said. "Let's put a stop to this."

"Go away, you rude woman!" shouted Floradora.

The church hall went deathly quiet. Everyone would have liked to laugh but did not dare.

Mrs Bagg-Meanly was furious.

"Vicar!" she roared. "Get this shameless creature off my stage!"

"Shoo!" said Mr Snelling weakly.

"Shoo yourself," replied Floradora. "How dare you speak like that to a STAR?"

But someone else was climbing onto the stage. It was Ted Bleinkinsop and he was very angry.

"Star, my foot!" he snapped. "That's no Divine Floradora – that's Nellie, my best cow!"

"I am no longer your cow," said Floradora. "I am an artiste."

This made Ted Blenkinsop even angrier.

"Take all that muck off your face, my girl, and come home to your pasture!"

"No–o–o–o–o!" cried the cow in a long moo.

"Do as you're told," said Ted Blenkinsop. "No cow of mine goes prancing about on stage like a painted hussy."

Careful not to be noticed, Mr Babbercorn slipped out of the church hall. He was just in time. Old Noshie and Skirty Marm had climbed off the roof and were trying to sneak away.

"Stop right there!" ordered Mr Babbercorn.

The witches stopped.

"I hope you're both ashamed of yourselves," said Mr Babbercorn. "You're certainly a disappointment to me."

These were terrible words. Old Noshie and Skirty Marm hung their heads sulkily.

"Do you realize what you've done?" Mr Babbercorn demanded. "Nellie is Mr Blenkinsop's favourite cow – worth a lot of money and almost one of the family. She was perfectly happy until you two came along and filled her head with silly ideas. Remove that spell at once."

The witches scowled and looked at their toes.

"It was only a joke," mumbled Skirty Marm.

"You were mean to us," said Old Noshie. "We wanted to teach you a lesson."

"The only lesson you have taught me," said Mr Babbercorn, "is that I can't trust you."

He grasped them each by their bony hands so they could not escape and marched them round to the side of the church hall. The Divine Floradora was already outside. The concert had broken up in chaos, and she was sitting in the middle of the path, refusing to budge.

"Blast it all, Nellie!" Ted Blenkinsop was shouting. "Why won't you come home?"

"Because I'm going to Hollywood to be a film star," said Floradora. "I'm bored with the farm."

"Bored!" cried Ted Blenkinsop. "Well, there's gratitude for you. I've given you everything. You've had the best field, the longest grass . . . "

Mr Babbercorn parked the witches in the laurel bushes.

"Stay there," he said, "and when I nod to you, take off the spell."

He went over to the cow and put his arm around her neck.

"Now, Nellie, listen to me," he said. "Don't you think it would be wiser to stay in Tranters End?"

"No," said the cow. "And don't call me Nellie. I'm Floradora, the Bovine Marvel."

"You've never known any other life," Mr Babbercorn said gently. "I think you'd soon want your home. And what about poor Mr

Blenkinsop? Think how he'd miss you. Not to mention Mrs Blenkinsop and the children."

"That's right, Nellie," said Ted Blenkinsop. "Why, if you left us it would ruin our Christmas!"

The Divine Floradora sighed. "I've been a very silly girl. How could I think of leaving my dear family? Please take me home so I can just be Nellie again!"

"That's my lass," said Ted Blenkinsop. He gave her the kind of slap on the flank that cows like.

Mr Babbercorn nodded to the witches. A few seconds later, Nellie mooed loudly. The spell had been removed and she was an ordinary cow again.

"What a relief!" Mr Blenkinsop mopped his red face. "Thanks for talking some sense into her, Mr Babbercorn. I don't know what we'd do, without our Nellie."

The Blenkinsop family led their beloved cow home.

Skirty Marm tugged at Mr Babbercorn's sleeve.

"We still think you're mean!" she announced. "You can't take a joke and you won't let us have any fun. We don't want to be your friends any more."

"So POOH TO YOU!" added Old Noshie.

The two witches stuck out their tongues and vanished into thin air.

Mr Babbercorn went very sadly back to the vicarage.

I was absolutely right to tell them off, he thought. They knew they were being naughty. But, oh dear – whatever shall I do without them?

8

Witches to the Rescue

Old Noshie and Skirty Marm were deeply offended by Mr Babbercorn's strict words. He had hurt their feelings when he said he could not trust them. For the next three days they stayed sulking in their belfry, waiting for the curate to climb the one hundred and eighty-six steps and say he was sorry.

But the days passed, and Mr Babbercorn did not come.

"What did I tell you?" sniffed Skirty Marm. "He doesn't love us any more. Let's go right back to being bad."

"It'll serve him right," said Old Noshie. "He'll have to come and see us then."

The moment it was dark, they flew out on their brooms for a game of Vests-in-the-Rain.

There was hardly any washing hanging out on the December evening so the game was not much fun. They shouted "Pooh to you!" down a few chimneys, but took no relish in it. And when they returned to the belfry, sure that Mr Babbercorn would come rushing to tell them off, they were disappointed. Not even severe naughtiness had brought the curate.

"We're obviously not being bad enough," growled Skirty Marm. "We'll have to think of something worse."

"Being good was certainly very tiring," admitted Old Noshie. "But I miss our friend, Skirt. Don't you?"

"No!" said Skirty Marm. But she did not sound very sure.

"You know what, Skirt?" Old Noshie went on bravely. "I think we should go to see him. I think we're the ones who should say sorry. After all, we were pretty naughty."

"Pish and posh," said Skirty Marm proudly. "Let him apologize to us!"

"But, Skirt," Old Noshie wailed, "what if he doesn't?"

Skirty Marm thought hard. She did not want to lose their only friend, and she was secretly longing for an excuse to make it up.

"All right," she said at last. "Let's go to see

him. After all, it is nearly Christmas."

"Hurrah!" cried Old Noshie.

The witches had been very bored and lonely without Mr Babbercorn and, deep down, they knew he had been right to tell them off. Though they would never have admitted it, being bad was not as much fun as they remembered.

The minute the high street was empty, the witches flew over to the vicarage and climbed through Mr Babbercorn's bedroom window.

"Skirt, look!" whispered Old Noshie.

There, lying pale and ghastly on his lumpy bed, was the poor curate. He was so thin he looked like his own shadow.

"Oh, Mr B.!" cried Skirty Marm. "What has happened to you?"

"Witches!" Mr Babbercorn said weakly. "It's lovely to see you, but you shouldn't be here – you're in danger . . ."

"We came to say sorry," said Old Noshie in a small voice. "We'll be good for ever now. Won't we, Skirt?"

"Yes," gulped Skirty Marm.

"Old Noshie and Skirty Marm," said Mr Babbercorn, "I'm afraid I'm very ill. Mrs Bagg-Meanly has done for me at last! She made me eat

something poisonous, and I'm sinking fast – starvation has undermined my constitution. You have been wonderful friends. Please be kind to the vicar, for my sake."

"We'll make you fly again," promised Old Noshie. "We'll go back to your birthday island and build you a little house, and you'll be right as rain in no time."

Mr Babbercorn shook his head. "No use now. Goodbye, my dear witches. Be good, and don't forget me."

Big tears rolled down the faces of the two witches. As they flew back to the belfry they were bitterly sorry they had ever been cross with their friend.

"If only we could do something to help him!" sobbed Old Noshie. "He called us his dear witches!"

"Stop howling," said Skirty Marm, "I'm trying to think of a spell."

"There's no spell strong enough for this," said Old Noshie. "Not even in the Purple-Stocking Spellbook. It's quite useless!"

But Skirty Marm was having profound and important thoughts.

"There is one spell that would help Mr Babbercorn," she said. "MRS ABER-CROMBIE'S PRIVATE POTION!"

Old Noshie's green face turned pale. "You're a loony! The recipe's in her special spellbook – it's impossible!"

"It's our only hope," said Skirty Marm quietly. "We have to get it."

"But how, Skirt, how?" Old Noshie was shaking all over with horror.

"We'll have to fly back to Witch Island and steal it," said Skirty Marm. "We'll go tonight, when she's asleep, and look up the spell in her book. She'll never know we were there."

"What about her guards?"

"We'll biff them and tie them up," said Skirty Marm firmly.

"Biff them?" shrieked Old Noshie. "How are we going to biff huge old Purple-Stocking palace guards?"

"Suit yourself," Skirty Marm said loftily. "I'll do it on my own."

Old Noshie remembered Mr Babbercorn calling them "dear witches", and suddenly felt very brave.

"You're right – we have to take the chance. Even if we get our noses squashed," she added in a wobbly voice.

Night fell upon Tranters End. It was freezing cold and extremely dark. Their hearts thumping, the witches set out on their quest to save their friend. Never had the little village seemed so cosy and welcoming. Never had the thought of Mrs Abercrombie seemed so awful.

After several hours of fast flying they saw the looming black mountains of Witch Island. They landed silently, on the sooty beach nearest the palace, and hid their brooms under some black rocks. It felt very strange, returning to their old home which they had not expected to see for a hundred years. Although it was pitch dark, Old Noshie and Skirty Marm knew every stone by heart.

The entrance to the palace cave was guarded by four massive Purple-Stocking witches, each holding a flaming torch.

"The back door has guards on it, too," whispered Skirty Marm. "We'll have to go down the chimney."

"We must be mad!" grumbled Old Noshie. But she followed her friend up the rough sides of the royal cave. It was a steep and painful climb. By the time they reached the chimney, they were both bruised and panting.

"Oh, stinks!" swore Old Noshie, coughing in the smoke. "The fire's still lit – we'll be burned to a crisp! Now what shall we do?"

"We'll try to land in the coal bucket," said Skirty Marm grimly. "Don't be so wet, Nosh. I'm not going to turn back now."

"Wet, am I?" snarled Old Noshie. "I'll show you!" She grabbed Skirty Marm's hand.

"One, two, three . . . jump!" cried the witches together – and they leapt boldly down the palace chimney.

As luck would have it, they landed not in the coal bucket but smack on top of an old Purple-Stocking, who was snoring beside the fire. She was squashed as flat as a pancake and knocked unconscious. It was a promising start which cheered them both enormously.

"So far, so good," said Skirty Marm. "Now, let's find Mrs Abercrombie's bedroom!"

They tiptoed through the damp, rocky corridors, following the sound of the queen's huge, rumbling snores, which shook the earth beneath their feet.

As they approached the chamber where Mrs Abercrombie lay sleeping, their teeth chattered with fear – they were not even pretending to be brave. Four more guards stood outside the queen's bed-cave, their hairy faces glaring in the light of their torches.

"It's impossible!" moaned Old Noshie.

"Shhh!" ordered Skirty Marm. "I'm thinking!"

At that moment, from a distant quarter of the great palace cave, a voice called, "Two o'clock, and all's well!"

The voice bounced off the dank stone walls, echoing and re-echoing for ages until it seemed to come from a thousand places at once.

"That's it!" exclaimed Skirty Marm. "We'll trick them!" She dragged Old Noshie into a narrow cranny in the wall.

"Ow!" complained Old Noshie. "What are you playing at?"

To her astonishment and horror, Skirty Marm threw back her head and yelled as loud as she could, "Help! Burglars! Help! Robbers! Crocodiles! Help!"

Her voice swooped and dived as if hundreds of Skirty Marms were yelling at once all over the palace.

The effect on the four guards was dramatic.

"It's over there—"

"No, over here—"

"This way, I tell you—"

They scattered in four different directions, leaving the door to the royal bed-cave unguarded.

Old Noshie and Skirty Marm wasted no time. The moment the guards were out of sight, they scuttled through the curtained archway.

"Yeuch!" Skirty Marm said feelingly.

Mrs Abercrombie lay snoring on her massive granite bed, the fat rippling all over her gigantic body. The last time the witches had seen her was at their trial. She was terrible to look upon, and the thought of poor Mr Babbercorn was all that kept them from running away.

In one corner of the gloomy cave stood a stone table. On that table lay a mighty book. They had never seen it before, but they knew only too well what it was – *Mrs Abercrombie's Private Collection of Spells*, the most magic and dangerous book in all the world.

As quietly as possible, Skirty Marm opened the vast book and began searching through the index of recipes. This was difficult because the pages were thin and crackly. However, she soon found what they had come for.

"Page 7777776," she whispered solemnly, "Mrs Abercrombie's Private Potion."

"Drat!" muttered Old Noshie, peering over her shoulder.

They had hoped just to glance at the spell and learn it by heart, but it covered a whole page of the book in tiny writing.

"Only one thing for it," said Old Noshie recklessly. "We'll have to tear the page right out and take it with us."

"Here goes!" Skirty Marm ripped out the

page and folded it safely inside her rags. "Done it!"

"YES!" rumbled a dreadful voice from the bed. "You've done it! Welcome back to Witch Island, you miserable little scoundrels!"

Mrs Abercrombie was sitting up on her cement pillows, with sparks fizzing out of her hideous mouth.

Old Noshie and Skirty Marm squealed.

"I'll boil you in oil for this!" roared Mrs Abercrombie. "How dare you steal my secret spells? Give back that page – I'm going to turn you into slugs, and I don't want tracks all over it!"

She raised her hand, and the witches gave themselves up for lost. It had all been for nothing, and they were about to become slugs.

Then, suddenly, Old Noshie shrieked, "She can't do anything – she's not wearing her hat! She's powerless without it! Run, Skirt, run!"

"Guards!" howled Mrs Abercrombie. "Where are my guards?"

Skirty Marm did a very brave thing. She ran right to the end of the queen's bed where the Power Hat hung on the bedpost, the everlasting candle burning in its point. Then she snatched the Power Hat and rammed it on her own head.

Mrs Abercrombie turned pale grey and crashed back on her bed in a dead faint. Without the Hat she was only an ordinary Purple-Stocking. Whoever wore the Power Hat was the rightful Queen of Witch Island. Her cruel reign was over.

Old Noshie and Skirty Marm dashed away down the long corridors, hooting with triumph. Time and time again the guards rushed at them, then fell back in dismay when they saw the flame of the magic hat.

"We did it!" shouted Old Noshie. "We did it!"

They ran to the beach, leapt on their brooms and zoomed away from Witch Island.

When they were well above the sea, Skirty Marm took off the Power Hat and flung it down into the waves.

Old Noshie was so staggered she almost toppled off her broom. "Why did you do that? You could have been Queen of Witch Island!"

"Pooh!" said Skirty Marm. "I don't ever want to go back there. It's a smelly place. It'll do them good to try democracy, for a change."

"Now we can stay in Tranters End for ever and ever!" said Old Noshie happily.

"Yes," said Skirty Marm. "If only . . . Oh, we haven't a minute to lose!"

9

What Happened at the Jumble Sale

There was only one hour of darkness left when the witches got back to Tranters End. Quickly, they flew among woods and hedges, picking all the herbs and berries they needed to make up Mrs Abercrombie's special potion.

Some of the ingredients were extremely strange, however, and far more difficult to find.

"'One churchwarden's toenail,'" read Old Noshie, frowning at the torn piece of paper.

"Mr Noggs is a churchwarden," said Skirty Marm.

They flew to the bedroom above the butcher's shop where Mr Noggs lay fast asleep beside his wife. Old Noshie cast a short-term sleeping spell (very simple, from the Yellow-Stocking Spell-book) and Skirty Marm pushed back Mr Noggs's duvet to snip off the nail of his left big toe.

The next ingredient on the list – "one hair of

a maiden in love" – was even easier. Belinda Tucker, the grown-up daughter of the Tuckers at the post office, was about to marry PC Bloater. The witches simply popped into the post office and plucked out one of Belinda's long brown hairs.

For "one reflection of an infant smile" they flew to Blodge Farm and caught the sweet smile of Matthew, the Blenkinsop baby, in a mirror.

The two witches were very determined and soon there was only one ingredient left on the list.

"'A stamp'," read Old Noshie, "'that has been licked by someone with a black heart'."

"Ha!" said Skirty Marm. "I know who has a black heart around here."

"Mrs Bagg-Meanly!" cried Old Noshie.

They flew to the bedroom window of the black-hearted housekeeper. She lay, snoring loudly, beneath a pink quilt with half a chocolate cake on the bedside table.

"You do the sleeping spell," said Skirty Marm, "and I'll get the window open. She must have a stamp around somewhere – we'll just wipe it against her tongue."

"Yuck!" grumbled Old Noshie. "I'm not doing that!"

She did not have to. On the table lay a letter, in Mrs Bagg-Meanly's writing, with a stamp already licked and stuck on the envelope. Skirty Marm snatched it, and the two friends rushed back to the belfry just as the sun was rising.

"Bother, we haven't got a cauldron," muttered Skirty Marm. "We'll have to use your hat."

By the time the sun was properly up they were hard at work, boiling and brewing and racking their brains to remember everything they had learned at witch school. This was the toughest spell they had ever tried. One by one, they dropped the ingredients into the mixture bubbling away in Old Noshie's hat.

In the early afternoon, two exhausted witches sniffed the nasty-smelling mixture.

"All ready," announced Skirty Marm. "Come on, Nosh – I don't care if anyone sees us. This is an emergency."

In fact, everyone in the village had gone to Mrs Bagg-Meanly's Christmas jumble sale, so the streets were deserted when the witches zoomed over to the vicarage, clutching the precious hatful of medicine.

Mr Babbercorn lay as they had left him,

stretched out on his bed. He was so pale and still that the witches were frightened.

"Wake up!" cried Old Noshie. "It's us! We've come to make you better!"

Mr Babbercorn only groaned.

"Deary me," said Skirty Marm, "these humans are such delicate little creatures – a puff of wind could blow them away!"

She poured a few drops of the potion down the poor curate's throat. Holding their breaths, the witches waited.

"It doesn't work!" wailed Old Noshie, starting to grizzle.

"Look!" hissed Skirty Marm.

Slowly, a change was creeping over Mr Babbercorn. First, colour surged into his thin cheeks until they were quite red and round. Then his wispy hair became thick and yellow, and his skinny arms and legs swelled with muscle. Even his shabby clothes turned glossy and new. Altogether, he was more healthy and hearty than he had ever been in his life.

Old Noshie and Skirty Marm were so astonished by the power of the potion that they shrank back against the wall as Mr Babbercorn leapt off his bed.

"Good gracious!" he exclaimed "I feel *wonderful*!"

His voice had grown stronger, too – he no longer had a weedy tenor but a rich, deep bass-baritone.

"What a beautiful day!" He flung open the window – and he was so strong that the whole thing came away in his hand.

"Hurrah!" screamed Old Noshie and Skirty Marm, breaking into a dance of delight. "It worked!"

"My dear witches," said Mr Babbercorn in his new deep voice, "how has this happened? And how can I ever thank you?"

He lifted them both into the air with one finger so that their heads bumped against the ceiling. Once their feet were back on the floor, the witches told him how they had returned to Witch Island to steal Mrs Abercrombie's spell.

Mr Babbercorn was so touched by their bravery that big, juicy tears rolled down his face.

"You'll never be able to go back to your island again," he said, "and you did it all for me!"

"Because you're our friend," said Old Noshie

proudly, "And we never had a proper friend before – did we, Skirt?"

"You'll be able to give that Mrs Bagg-Meanly a good biffing now," said Skirty Marm. "We never dreamed this potion would be so good. We only used a teeny drop – there's tons left."

"Is there now?" Mr Babbercorn was thoughtful. "I've got an idea. Come with me."

He picked up the two witches as if they had been as light as two feathers and carried them down the vicarage stairs, one on each shoulder. As they crossed the landing, they heard the voice of Mrs Bagg-Meanly.

She was in her bedroom, chortling to herself and singing a horrid little song:

> "Har har harm, hee hee hee,
> I've poisoned him and now I'm free!
> Now this one's gone, I need not fear –
> THEY WON'T SEND NO MORE
> CURATES HERE!"

"We'll see about that!" said Mr Babbercorn.

As I have said, everyone in the village was at the jumble sale, by order of Mrs Bagg-Meanly. And a very gloomy jumble sale it was. Nobody spoke, but instead stood around the church hall in sad little groups. Mr Snelling sat behind the bric-a-brac stall, sniffing because he was so worried about his poor curate.

When Mr Babbercorn strode in, with a witch on each shoulder, there was a terrific sensation.

"Cuthbert!" gasped Mr Snelling. He jumped up so suddenly that he knocked over a "Present from Skegness" cruet on his stall. "Can this really be you?"

"It certainly is!" boomed Mr Babbercorn, gently putting down the witches.

The villagers gaped at him, unable to believe their eyes.

"But . . . but . . ." stammered Mr Snelling, "I left you lying ill in bed!"

"Well, now I'm cured," said Mr Babbercorn. "I'm as fit as a flea." To prove it, he lifted the whole bric-a-brac table in the air and held it above his head.

"Can this really be my poor young curate?" cried Mr Snelling. "Why, you're as strong as Superman!" The kind-hearted vicar blew his nose loudly, overcome with joy.

"Listen everybody," Mr Babbercorn said. "I'll explain everything later. Right now, we have work to do. We're going to overthrow the tyrant, Mrs Bagg-Meanly, and drive her out of this village for ever!"

There were murmurs of "Impossible!" and "He's gone crazy!" Tranters End without Mrs Bagg-Meanly seemed too good to be true.

While all this was going on, Old Noshie and Skirty Marm had been busy. Into the big tea urn at the back of the hall they poured the rest of Mrs Abercrombie's potion.

"You must all trust me," said Mr Babbercorn, "and do exactly as I say. First, everyone must have a cup of tea. Line up, please."

The villagers were too dazed by these strange happenings to protest. Besides, this new, dynamic curate was not the sort of person you disobeyed. They formed an orderly queue beside the urn, and Old Noshie and Skirty Marm served the tea. It had not been nice tea to begin with and the potion made it smell worse.

"Who are these two raggedy old ladies?" whispered Mrs Noggs to Mrs Tucker. "They look just like a couple of . . . well . . . witches!"

At precisely half past two, Mrs Bagg-Meanly entered the church hall. She was in high spirits, singing her little song and wondering what to wear to Mr Babbercorn's funeral. But she stopped short at the door for an extraordinary sight met her eyes.

They were all waiting for her, in a half-circle, not at all frightened. In fact, they were smiling. For the first time in her life, Mrs Bagg-Meanly felt uneasy. What could this mean?

Then two figures stepped forward. One was Mr Snelling and the other was—

"Argh!" screamed Mrs Bagg-Meanly, "You? What are you doing here? What's going on?"

She grabbed Mr Babbercorn's ear, but he

111

shook her off as if she had been a fly.

"What-what-what?" she choked, turning a ghastly colour. "I'm sending that poison straight back to the shop! It doesn't work and I've been tricked! Harold Snelling, I want an explanation!"

To her amazement, all Mr Snelling said was, "Shut up."

"What?" gasped Mrs Bagg-Meanly.

"I said, Shut up, Cousin Violet," said the vicar. "The worm has turned at last. You've made us all miserable for far too long. I'm in charge now – and this is my jumble sale!"

The villagers of Tranters End burst into a round of applause and there were cries of "Hear! hear!"

"So!" roared Mrs Bagg-Meanly. "You want me to lose my temper, do you?" She rolled up her sleeves, ready to fight for her power. "All right! Who wants to be first?"

"CHARGE!" shouted the vicar.

Before Mrs Bagg-Meanly knew what was happening, all the people of Tranters End were on top of her. They rolled her across the floor like a barrel, they tossed her in the air, they pinched and pummelled and tweaked and pulled, they messed up her hair and twanged her suspenders until she was shrieking for mercy.

"Stop! I'll do anything!"

"Cousin Violet," Mr Snelling said, "you have ruled Tranters End like a wicked tyrant. You have stolen my food and tried to poison my curate. But your reign of terror is over. You will pack your bags and go off to live with your sister. And if you ever set foot here again—"

"All right!" snarled Mrs Bagg-Meanly "You don't have to draw me a map, Harold. I'm going." She scrambled up, looking very sulky. "But you'll miss me – you wait and see!"

She stomped back to the vicarage to pack her bags and that was the last time her size eleven feet were ever heard in Tranters End.

There was a moment of stunned silence. Then someone shouted, "Three cheers for Mr Babbercorn!"

The cheers were so loud that the crockery on the bric-a-brac stall rattled.

Mr Babbercorn held up his hand for quiet. "Ladies and gentlemen," he said, "it isn't me you should be cheering today. Our village has been saved by two noble witches." He pulled forward Old Noshie and Skirty Marm, who blushed and looked very shy. "Old Noshie and Skirty Marm sheltered here when they were banished from their home. They risked being turned into slugs to get the magic potion that has done such wonders. Three cheers for Old Noshie and Skirty Marm!"

"Hip, hip, hurrah! Hurrah! Hurrah!" cheered everyone.

The two witches had never felt so proud and happy. They had once been wicked and played tricks on humans. Now here they were, being clapped and cheered and shaken by the hand. It was a lovely feeling.

"Why, being good is best after all!" said Old Noshie.

"I've always wanted to meet a real witch," said Mrs Tucker.

Ted Blenkinsop said, "Now I know what came over my Nellie!"

"Yes, it explains a lot," agreed Mr Snelling. "I knew a shrinking housekeeper and a singing cow couldn't be normal."

"Tell you what," cried Mr Noggs, who besides being a churchwarden was a butcher, "the vicar and Mr Babbercorn and these two magnificent witches will have the best Christmas dinner this village has ever seen! My biggest turkey . . ."

"And a big box of luxury crackers," chimed in Mrs Tucker.

"And a prize-winning pudding!" cried someone else.

Everyone began to offer delicious things to eat and drink until the hungry vicar's mouth was watering.

"You know what, Nosh?" said Skirty Marm. "I'm glad we were banished!"

"Me too," declared Old Noshie. "This is our real home now. And the humans are right – *East, West, Home's Best*!"

Kate Saunders
BELFRY WITCHES 2
Mendax the Mystery Cat

Old Noshie and Skirty Marm have been trying terribly hard to be
good. They've only done the tiniest bit of magic, they haven't
touched a drop of Nasty Medicine, and they've even been
learning how to knit!

But strange powers are at work in Tranters End. First there's the
underwear that comes to life, then the flying pigs – and then a
very mysterious black cat arrives at the vicarage door . . .

Kate Saunders
BELFRY WITCHES 3
Red Stocking Rescue

Old Noshie and Skirty Marm are terribly upset. Although they've promised to be good, Mr Babbercorn won't let them be bridesmaids at his wedding. And Mendax the cat isn't even allowed to sing a solo!

But then deep, dark magic turns Alice, Mr Babbercorn's bride-to-be, into a snail. Who is the culprit – and can two brave witches (and one clever cat) cook up a spell that will save the wedding from disaster?

Collect all the BELFRY WITCHES books!

The prices shown below are correct at the time of going to press.
However, Macmillan Publishers reserve the right to show new retail
prices on covers which may differ from those previously advertized.

KATE SAUNDERS

1. A Spell of Witches	0 330 37282 3	£2.99
2. Mendax the Mystery Cat	0 330 37283 1	£2.99
3. Red Stocking Rescue	0 330 37284 X	£2.99
4. Power Hat Panic	0 330 37285 8	£2.99

All Macmillan titles can be ordered at your local bookshop
or are available by post from:

**Book Service by Post
PO Box 29, Douglas, Isle of Man IM99 1BQ**

Credit cards accepted. For details:
Telephone: 01624 675137
Fax: 01624 670923
E-mail: bookshop@enterprise.net

Free postage and packing in the UK.
Overseas customers: add £1 per book (paperback)
and £3 per book (hardback).